DARING DOG and CAPTAIN CAT

by ARNOLD ADOFF

illustrated by JOE CEPEDA

SIMON & SCHUSTER BOOKS FOR YOUNG READERS
New York London Toronto Sydney Singapore

SIMON & SCHUSTER BOOKS FOR YOUNG READERS
An imprint of Simon & Schuster Children's Publishing Division
1230 Avenue of the Americas, New York, New York 10020

Book design by Kristina Albertson
The text of this book is set in 17-point Bernhard Gothic Ultra.
The illustrations are rendered in oil paint.
Printed in Hong Kong
10 9 8 7 6 5 4 3 2 1
Library of Congress Cataloging-in-Publication Data
Adoff, Arnold.
Daring Dog and Captain Cat / by Arnold Adoff : illustrated by Joe Cepeda. — 1st ed.
p. cm.
Summary: Although they are normal and obedient pets during the day, at night Irving Dog and Ermine Cat rise and shake and roam as Daring Dog and Captain Cat, twirling capes and flashing swords and chasing crooks.
ISBN 0-689-82599-4 (hc)
[1. Dogs—Fiction. 2. Cats—Fiction. 3. Pets—Fiction.] I Cepeda, Joe, ill. II. Title.
PZ7.A2616Dar 2001 [E]—dc21 98-52885
first edition

Captain Cat
Still
Roams
The Long
Ohio
Night
—A. A.

For Cookie, Cleo, and the others
—J. C.

Dog Is Dog

And
Cat Is Cat
And We Are
Irving
Dog
And Ermine
Cat
On Our Tags
And Bowls
And
Cushion Beds

Our Children Give Us Those Names

But We Do Not Have Those Names
Inside
Our
Dog
And
Cat
Heads

They Give Us Homes

And Walk Us With
Bright Colored
Collars And
Long Leather Leads

They Call And Pet
AndPlay
They Feed Us
From
FullBowls

Come
Here Good Irving Dog
They
Say
Go
There Shy Ermine Cat

Come Chew This Bone
Come Let Me Pet Your
Head
Come Let Me
Comb The Burrs
Out Of Your
H a i r y Tail

We
Always
Come

With
Out
Fail

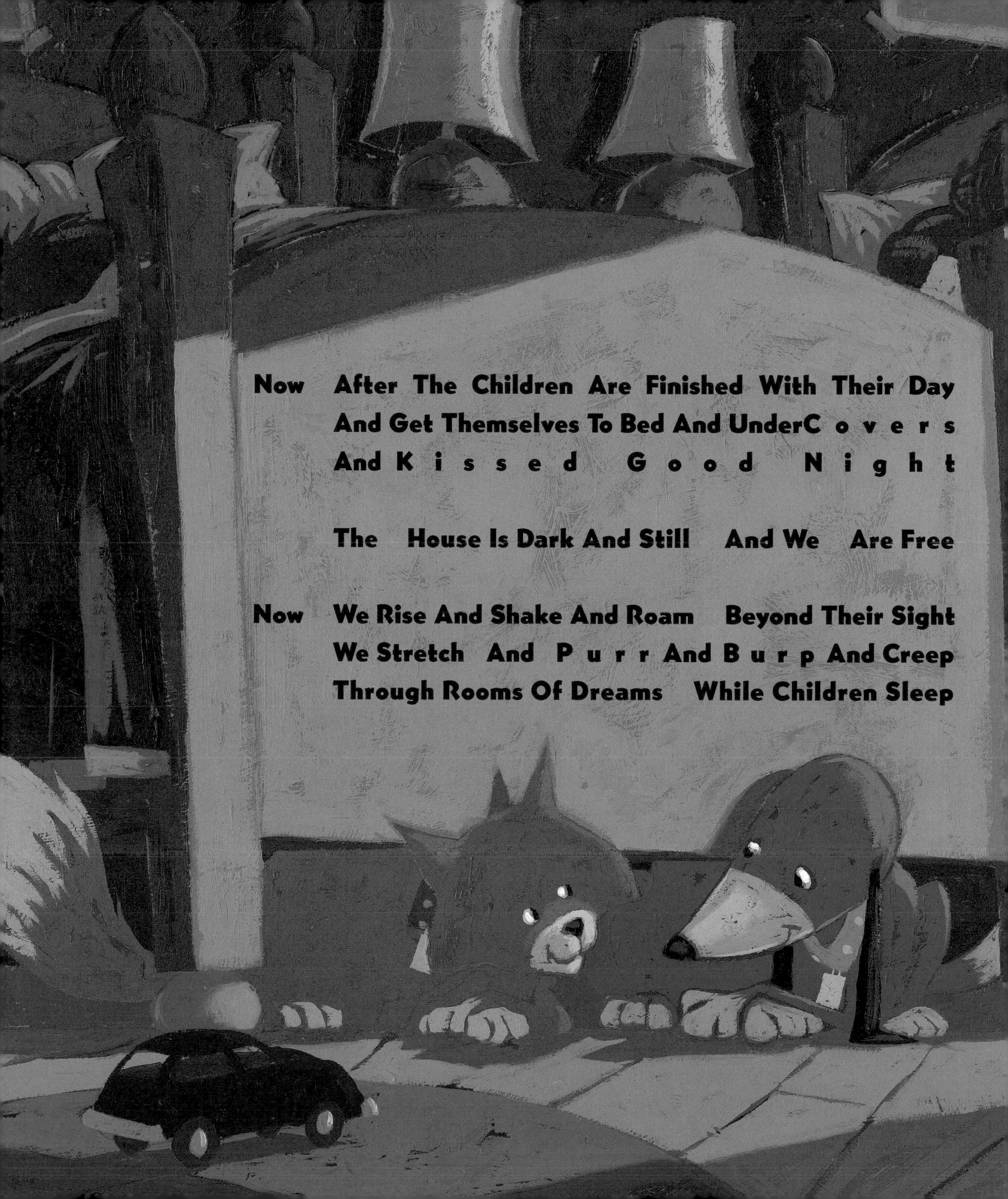

Now After The Children Are Finished With Their Day
And Get Themselves To Bed And UnderC o v e r s
And K i s s e d G o o d N i g h t

The House Is Dark And Still And We Are Free

Now We Rise And Shake And Roam Beyond Their Sight
We Stretch And P u r r And B u r p And Creep
Through Rooms Of Dreams While Children Sleep

We Are Daring Dog

And
Captain Cat
And
When We
Meet We
Raise Our
Paws
To
Reach The
Feather
At The Brim Of
Each
Imaginary Hat
And
Bend To
Bow So
Slightly
From The Waist

Then Daring Dog

Will Show His Canine Teeth
And Twirl His Purple Cape

Then Captain Cat

Will Grin Her Feline Grin
And Flash Her Silver Sword

And We Will Step In
To

Our
Oldest Dueling
Chasing
Dog
Cat
R a c e
Around T h e Room

We Move So Fast
We Flash

And
Fly
And Hiss And Bark
And Scratch
And Crawl
And Hide
And Hide
And Crawl Beside
The
Sofa
Or
Along The Wall

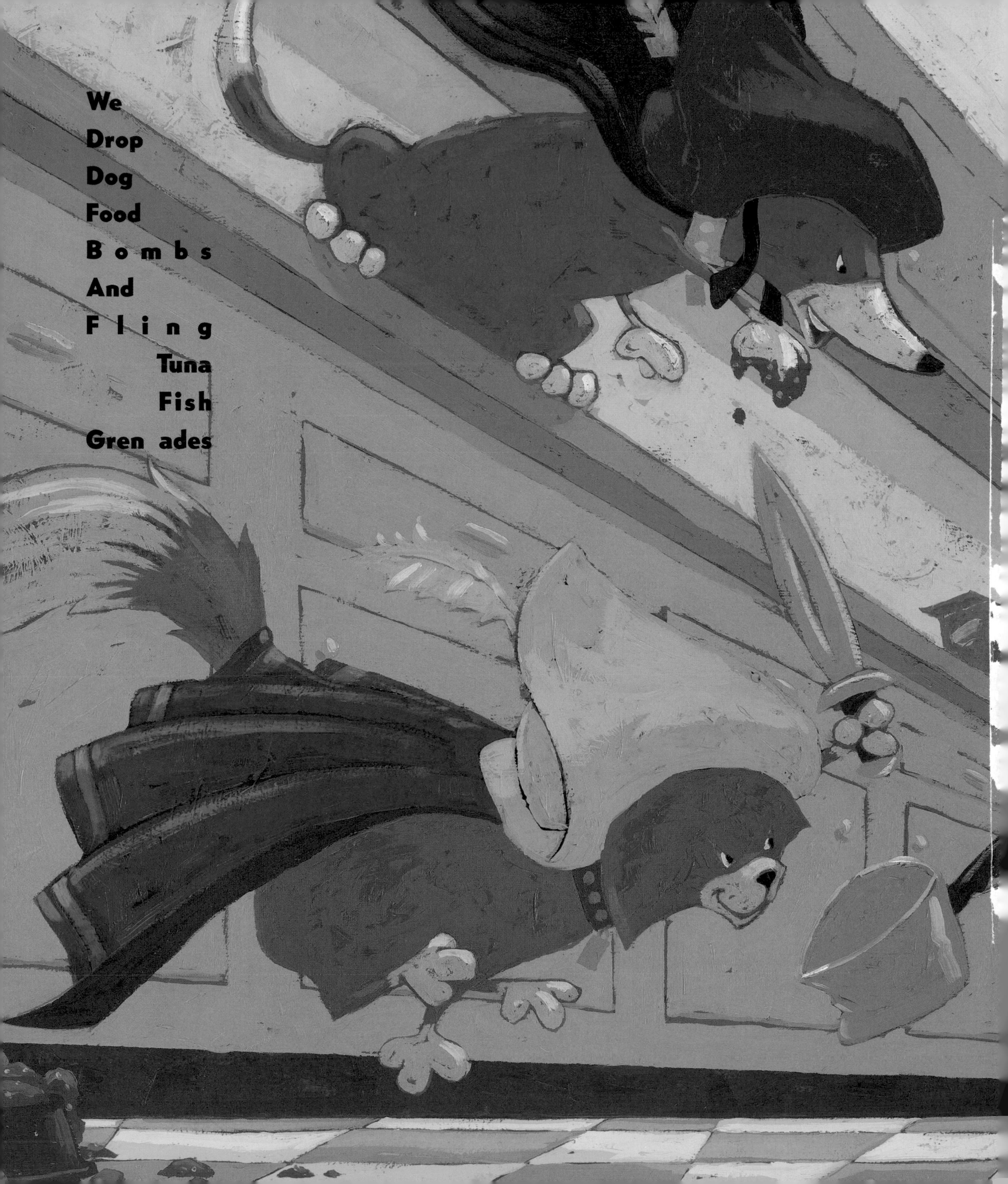

We
Drop
Dog
Food
Bombs
And
Fling
Tuna
Fish
Grenades

We Chase Each Other

And
Any Mindless M o u s e
Who Gets Too C l o s e
To
Any R a w h i d e Bone
Or C a t n i p Ball
Inside
The
Night
Rooms
Of Our H o u s e

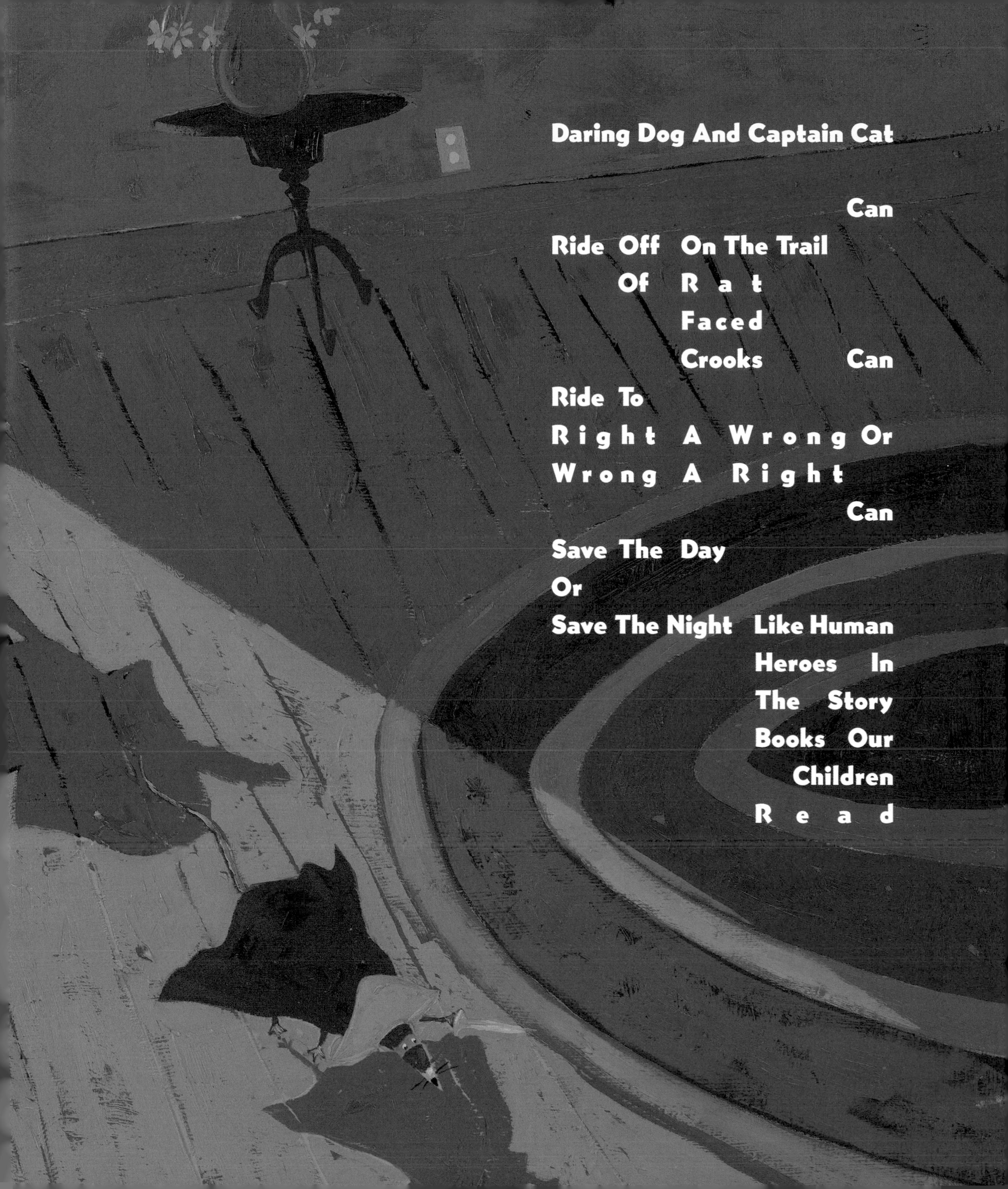

Daring Dog And Captain Cat

Can

Ride Off On The Trail

Of R a t

Faced

Crooks Can

Ride To

R i g h t A W r o n g Or

W r o n g A R i g h t

Can

Save The Day

Or

Save The Night Like Human

Heroes In

The Story

Books Our

Children

R e a d

We Twirl Our Capes
We Swirl Our Swords
We Race Like Horses
Charging
Through
The
Dark

We Show Our Teeth
We Almost Bite
We Fly OurPillows
Fighting
Through
The
Dark

Until We Crash

And Wreck This
Oldest L a m p
In
One
Gigantic
Boom
Of
Broken
Glass
And
Flash
And
Spark

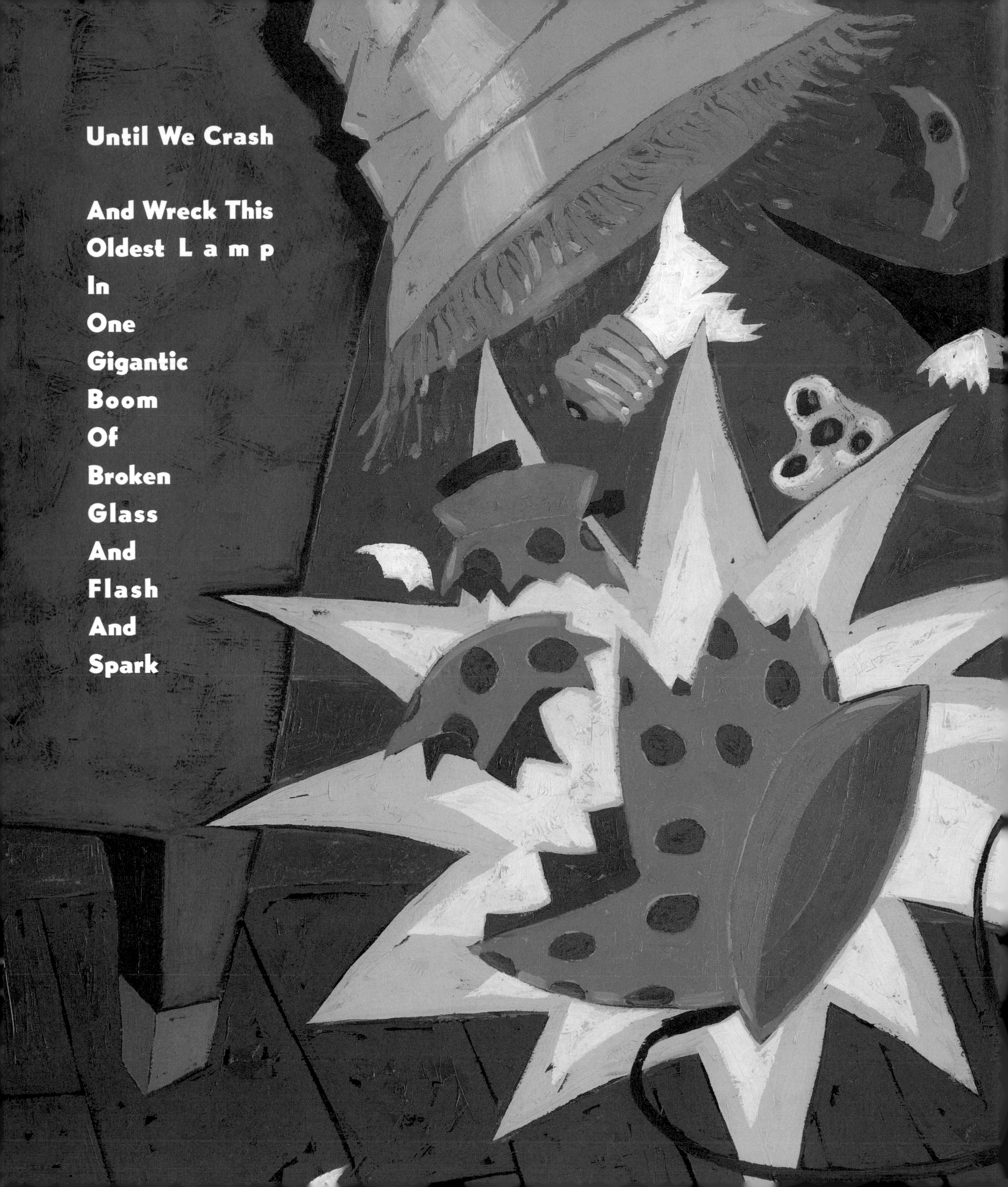

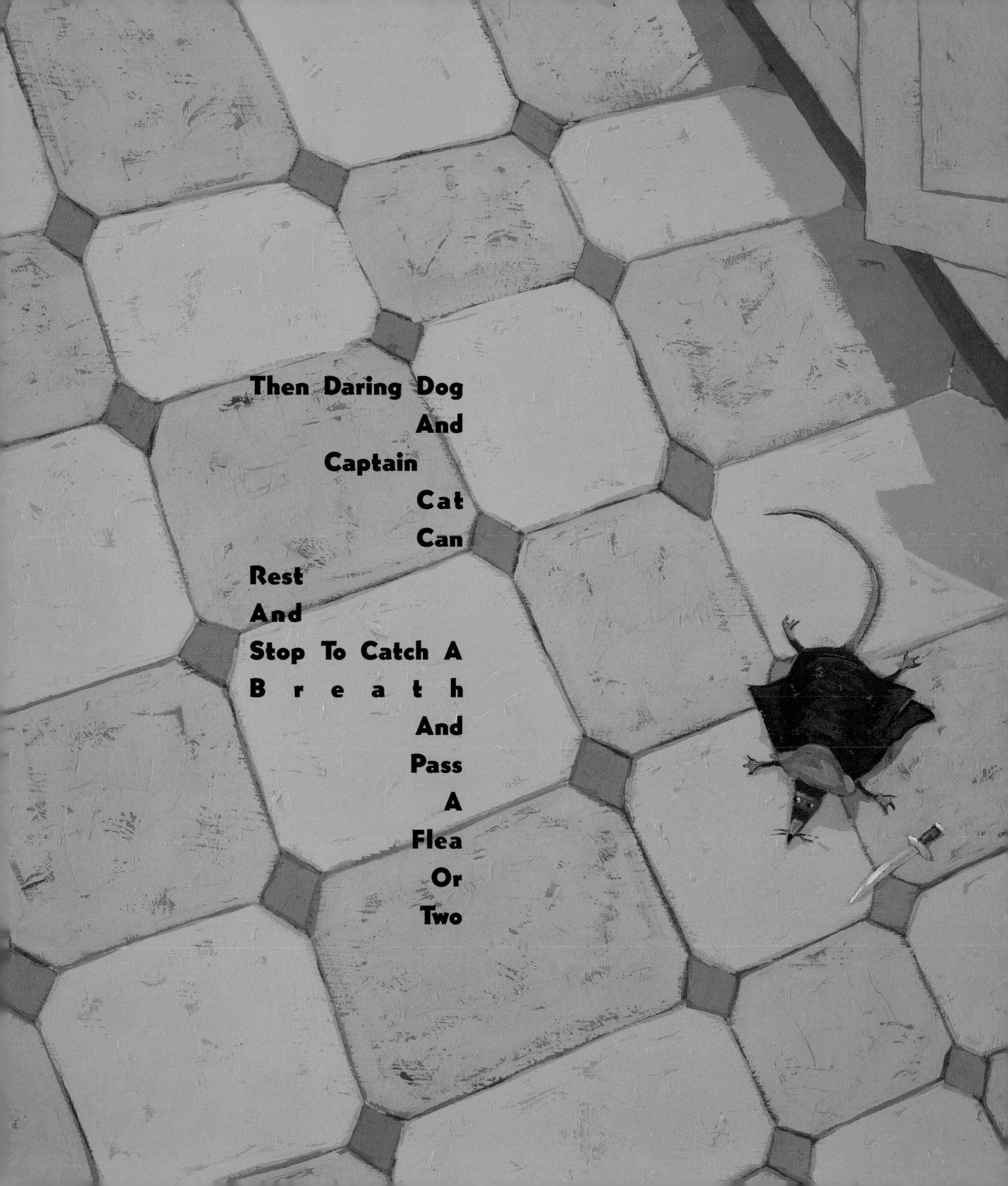

Then Daring Dog
And
Captain
Cat
Can
Rest
And
Stop To Catch A
Breath
And
Pass
A
Flea
Or
Two

And
Say How
Did
We
Do Tonight

Until The Early
MorningSun Comes
In
To
Wake Us
Slowly For
The
Day

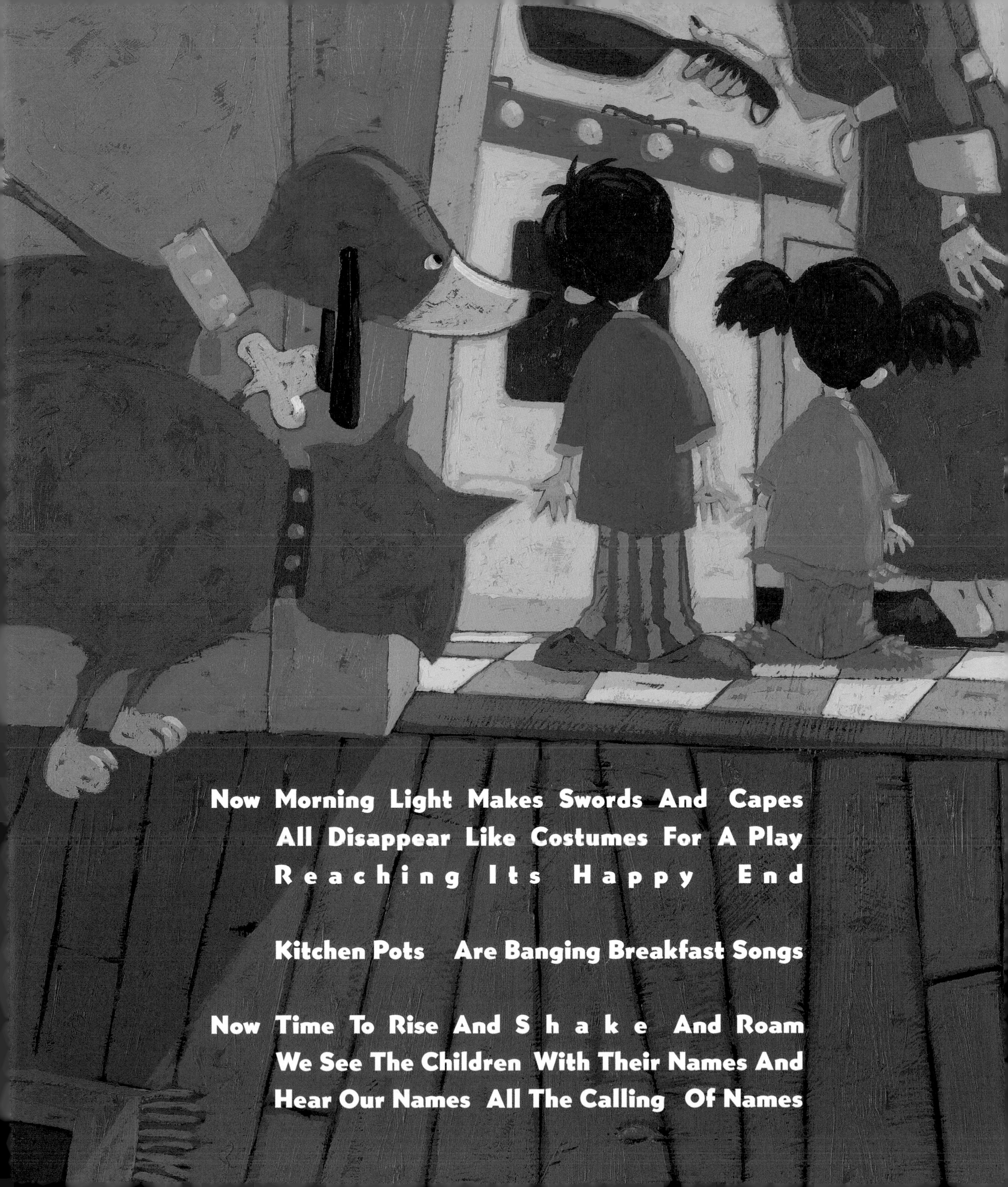

Now Morning Light Makes Swords And Capes
All Disappear Like Costumes For A Play
R e a c h i n g I t s H a p p y E n d

Kitchen Pots Are Banging Breakfast Songs

Now Time To Rise And S h a k e And Roam
We See The Children With Their Names And
Hear Our Names All The Calling Of Names

Good
Morning
Dog

Good
Morning
Cat

Come
Here Good Irving Dog
They
Say

Go
There Shy Ermine Cat

Come Chew This Bone
Come Let Me Pet Your
Head
Come Let Me
Comb The Burrs
Out Of Your
H a i r y Tail

We
Always
Come

With
Out
Fail

Then
We Hide In Corners

Curling
And Pretending Sleep
On Playing Afternoons
But
They Still Creep Up
Singing
S i l l y
S o n g s

They Give Us Hugs
And Look For Licks
And W h i s k e r
R u b b i n g
P u r r s

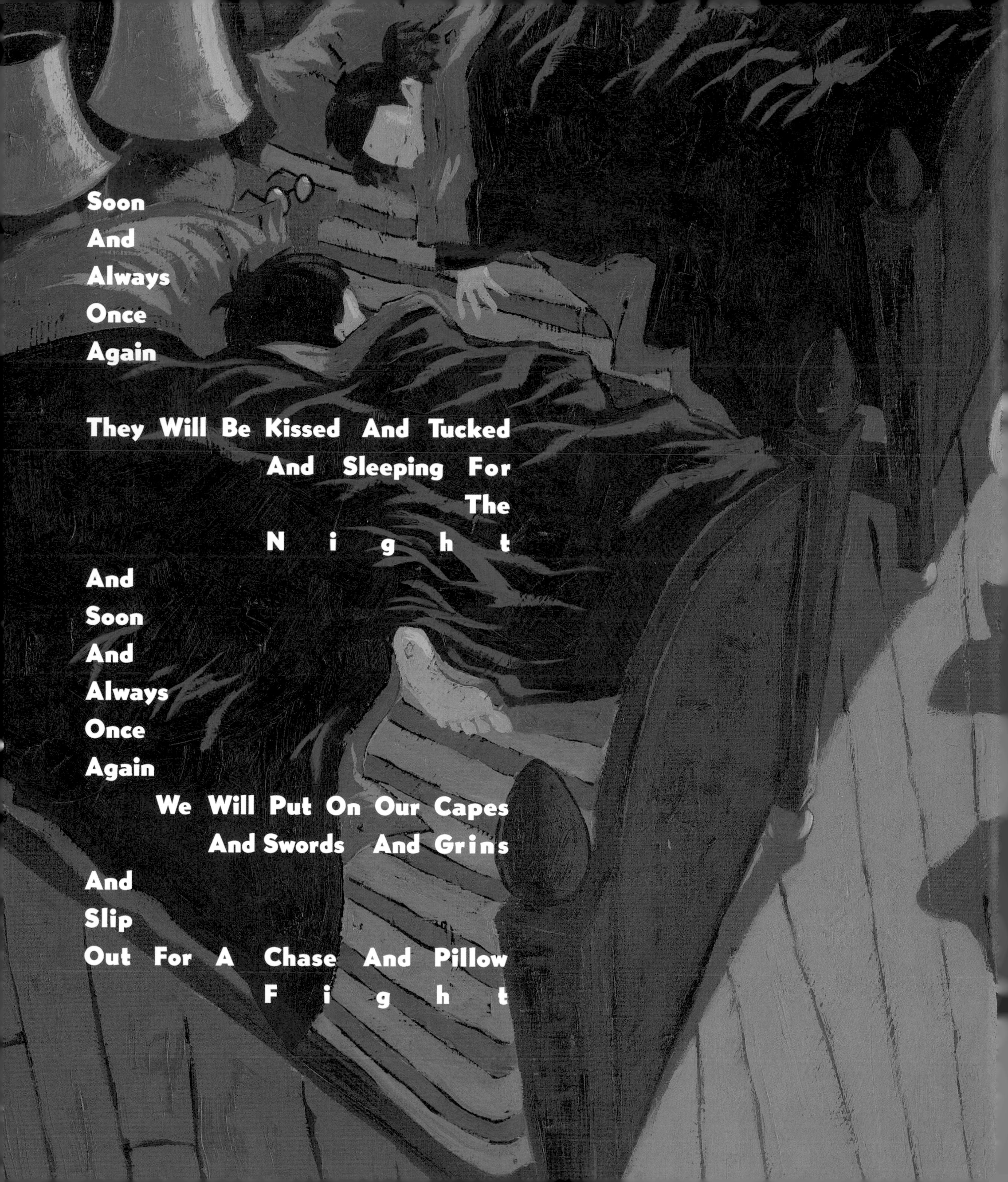

Soon
And
Always
Once
Again

They Will Be Kissed And Tucked
And Sleeping For
The
N i g h t
And
Soon
And
Always
Once
Again
We Will Put On Our Capes
And Swords And Grins
And
Slip
Out For A Chase And Pillow
F i g h t

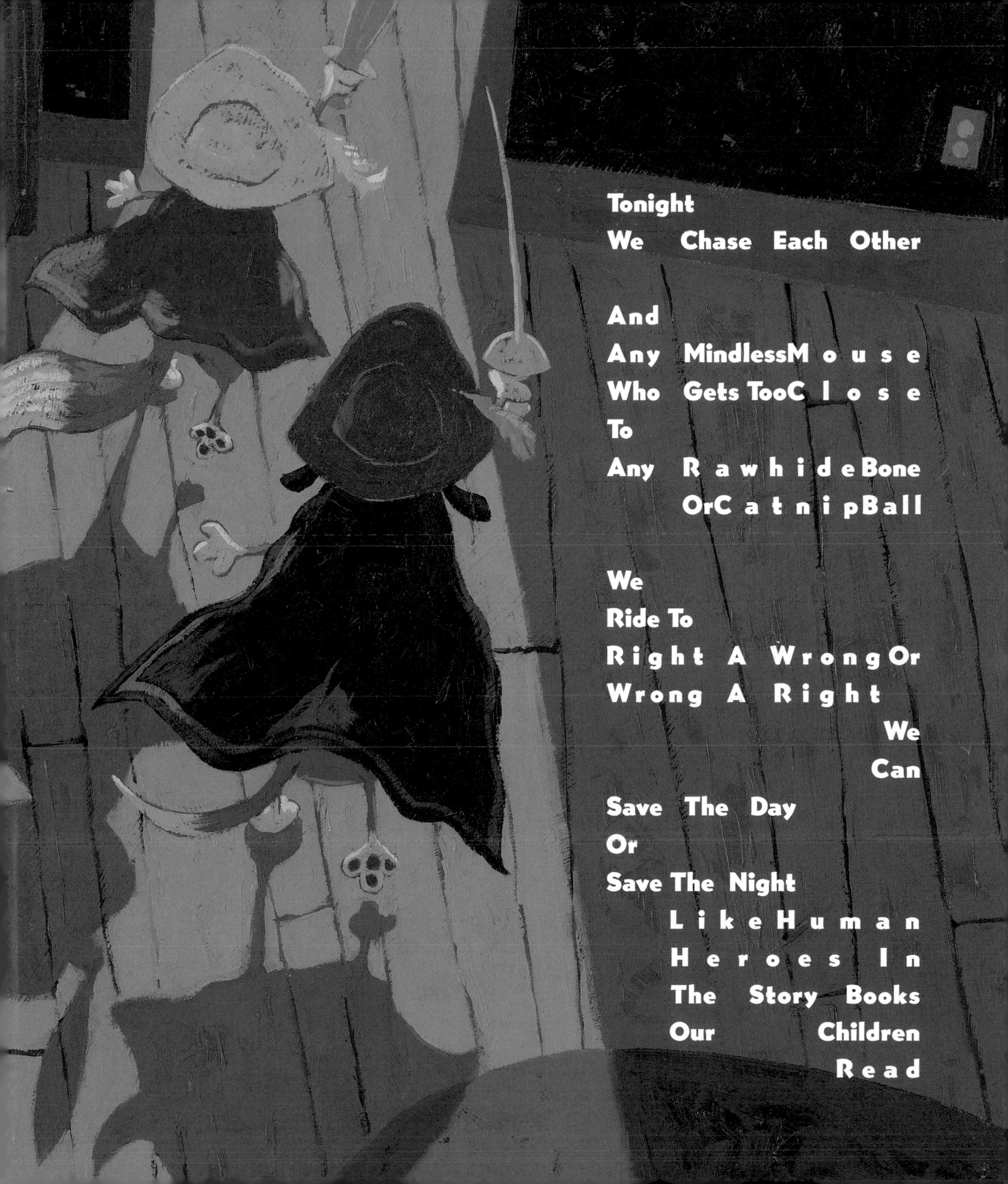

Tonight
We Chase Each Other

And
Any Mindless Mouse
Who Gets Too Close
To
Any Rawhide Bone
Or Catnip Ball

We
Ride To
Right A Wrong Or
Wrong A Right
We
Can
Save The Day
Or
Save The Night
Like Human
Heroes In
The Story Books
Our Children
Read

Irving Dog
And
Ermine Cat
Will
Always
Need
That
Dream
Will
Always Be
That
Team
Of
Daring Dog
And
Captain
Cat
Each Night

All
Sleep
Tight